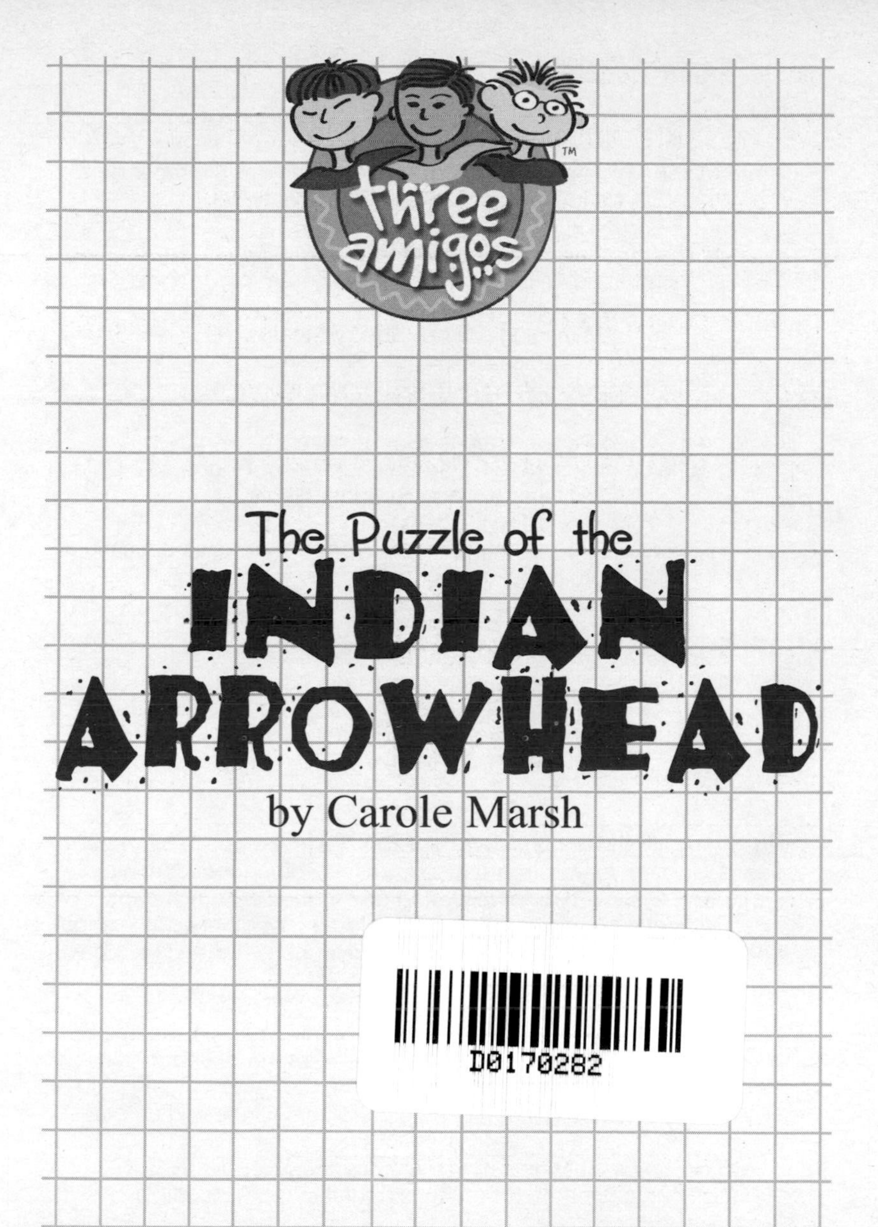

The Puzzle of the INDIAN ARROWHEAD

by Carole Marsh

First Edition

Carole Marsh Mysteries™ and its skull colophon are the property of
Carole Marsh and Gallopade International.

Published by Gallopade International/Carole Marsh Books.
Printed in the United States of America.

Managing Editor: Sherry Moss
Cover Design: Michele Winkelman
Illustration: Cecil Anderson, Yvonne Ford

Picture Credits: Carole Marsh
Photographs on pages 33, 34, and 35 courtesy of Roosevelt's Little
White House - Warm Springs, Georgia

Gallopade is proud to be a member and supporter of these educational
organizations and associations:
American Booksellers Association
International Reading Association
National Association for Gifted Children
The National School Supply and Equipment Association
The National Council for the Social Studies
Museum Store Association
Association of Partners for Public Lands

Dedicated to the "real"
Grant, Weng-Ho, and Seve.
Thank you for being such great
"characters."

A Word From the Author

Dear Reader,

Maybe you wonder how writers get their ideas? I got the idea for this book by watching three boys grow up together and become good friends, best buddies—and have a great time together! I think boys are really, really good at making friends for life, supporting one another, and sticking together in good times and in bad.

Join the Three Amigos as they learn about FDR and his life in Warm Springs, Georgia. Each year my husband and I attend a black tie ball fundraiser in Warm Springs and are always poignantly reminded of the good that was, and is, being done there.

Carole Marsh

About the Three Amigos

Weng-Ho, Grant, and Seve are best friends.

Weng-Ho is 7. Grant is 8. Seve is 9.

They live on the same street. Weng-Ho lives next door to Grant. Grant lives next door to Seve.

They go to the same school. Weng-Ho's classroom is next to Grant's. Grant's classroom is next to Seve's.

They each have a younger or older sister. Weng-Ho has a baby sister. Grant has an older sister. Seve has an even older sister.

They ride the school bus together. They eat lunch together. They go to recess together. Sometimes they get in trouble together. They like to solve riddles, mysteries, and puzzles together.

Or, at least they like to try!

The Case of the Crybaby Cowboy

The Riddle of the Oogli Boogli

The Puzzle of the Indian Arrowhead

TABLE OF CONTENTS

The Puzzle of the INDIAN ARROWHEAD

by Carole Marsh

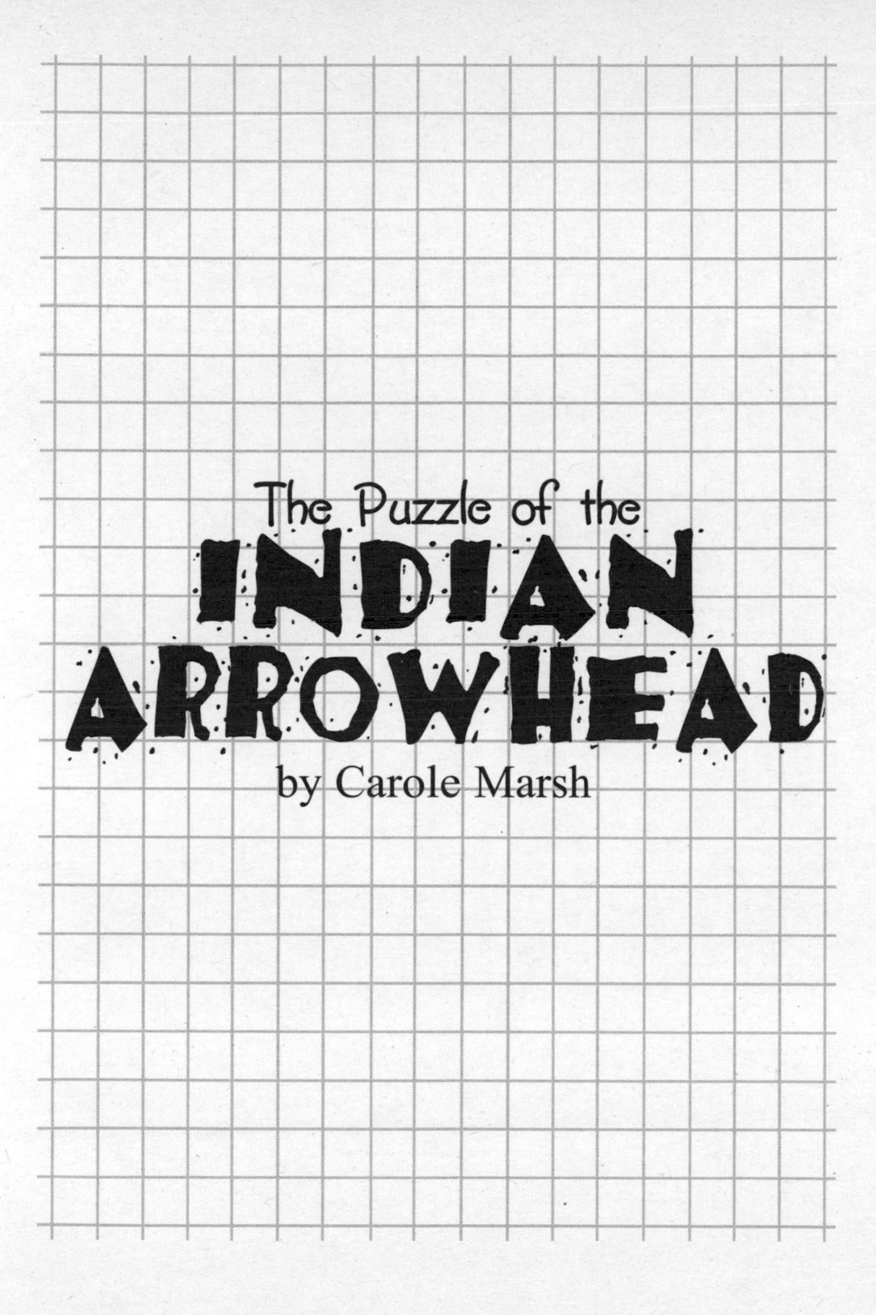

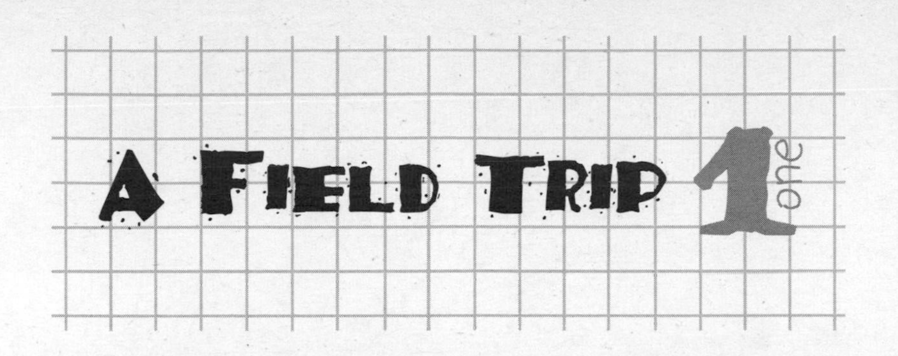

A Field Trip 1 one

It was a school holiday. Grant, Weng-Ho, and Seve were going on a field trip with Grant's dad, Mike. They were going to Warm Springs, Georgia. It was out in the country. The boys were very excited.

"What are we going to see, Dad?" asked Grant. His father was driving the van and the boys were all strapped into their seat belts. They looked out the window at the trees, and farms, and cows.

"We are going to see where FDR lived," said Mike.

"Who is FDR?" asked Weng-Ho.

"I know, I know!" said Seve. "His full name was Franklin Delano Roosevelt. He was a president of the United States of America."

"Very good!" said Mike.

"What else will we see, Dad?" asked Grant.

"We will see where the Creek Indians once lived," said Mike.

“Wow!” said Weng-Ho. “That sounds exciting.”

“What else will we see, Dad?” Grant asked.

“If we are lucky, we may find an Indian arrowhead,” said Mike.

“WOOOOOOW!” said the three amigos, all together.

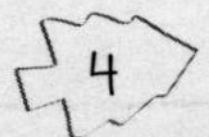
4

At last they came to a little town named Warm Springs. A sign pointed an arrow to The Little White House.

"That is where FDR lived," said Mike.

The boys looked puzzled. "But he was president," said Grant. "Why didn't he live at the big White House in Washington, D.C.,

like the other presidents?"

"He did," said Mike. "Most of the time. But when he was 39 years old, FDR got a disease. He got polio."

"What is polio?" asked Weng-Ho.

"Polio is a disease that cripples your legs, for one thing," said Mike. "It usually struck young children, but FDR got it. There was no cure. But he found that he could come soak in the warm springs and it made his legs feel better."

The boys looked sad.

"Can we go see the warm springs first?" asked Seve.

"Sure," said Mike. He made a sharp turn with the van.

Soon, they came to something that looked like swimming pools. The boys hopped out of the van. They ran and stuck their fingers in the water. It was warm—very warm.

"They must heat this pool?" asked Seve.

"No," said Mike. "The warm water comes from natural mineral springs. The water is warm in the winter and in the summer."

"Wow!" said the boys. They pulled off their shoes and stuck their toes in the water. It felt very warm and very good.

"Can we go see The Little White House now?" asked Grant.

The Little White House

3 three

They drove right up to The Little White House. It was little. It was white.

"This is not a very fancy house for a president," said Grant.

"No," said his dad. "But FDR did not want a fancy house here. He wanted a

place where he could rest and feel better."

They went inside. The house had a little living room and dining room. They saw the president's bedroom. They saw the kitchen. Then they saw a wheelchair sitting beside the back door.

"Did that belong to FDR?" asked Weng-Ho.

"Yes," said Mike. "Because his legs were crippled from polio, he had to use a wheelchair."

"So he was handicapped?" asked Seve.

Mike thought about that. "Yes," he finally said.

"But he was only handicapped in his legs. The rest of him was fine, and kind, and smart, and courageous. Most people never even knew he had polio."

"Wow!" said the boys.

"So who was president when FDR was here at The Little White House?" asked Seve.

"He was!" said Mike. "He would sit right here on the porch and do all his presidential business. He was a very good president. Living here in the Georgia countryside helped him understand the American people better. That way he knew how to help them."

"How did he do that?" asked Grant.

"Let's go see," said his dad.

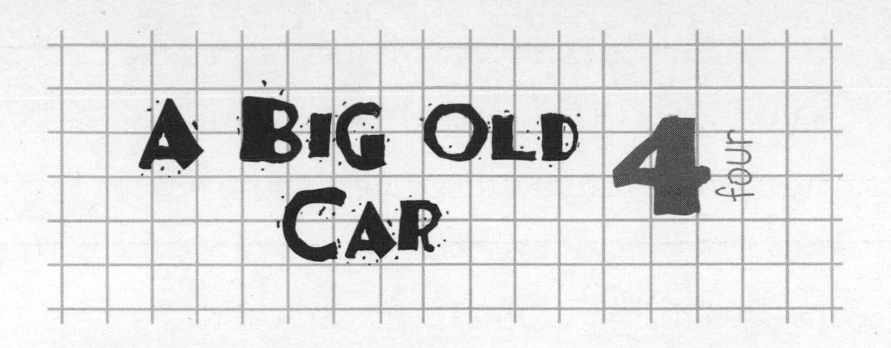

A Big Old Car

They went outside and saw the big, old car that FDR used to drive around Warm Springs. It was a convertible.

"If his legs had polio, how did he drive?" asked Grant.

"He had special things added to the

car so he could drive with just his hands," said Mike. "He drove all over Warm Springs visiting farmers and families."

"I'll bet they were excited to meet a president!" said Grant.

"Yes, they were," said Mike. "He learned what a hard time they were having during the Great Depression when there were no jobs and no money. He cared about them and designed programs to help all Americans."

"He seems like a nice man," said Seve.

"Yes, he was," said Mike.

"How did he get back and forth to the White House in Washington, D.C.?" asked Grant.

"Come on, I'll show you," said his dad.

NO WORK

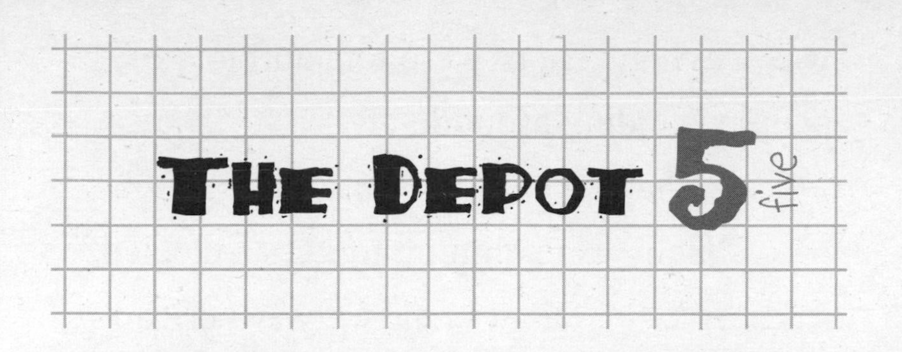

THE DEPOT 5 five

They drove to the Warm Springs train depot and went inside. There they saw pictures of big locomotives. They saw pictures of FDR on the back of the caboose. He

was waving. There were lots and lots of people standing around.

"What is he doing?" asked Seve.

"He is campaigning to get re-elected," said Mike. "FDR was the only American president elected to office four times!"

"Wow!" said Grant. "He must have really been popular."

"The people loved him," said his dad. "He gave them something very special."

"Money?" guessed Seve.

"No," said Mike.

"Jobs?" guessed Weng-Ho.

"No," said Mike

"Candy?" guessed Grant.

"No," said his dad. "I will let you figure out this puzzle for yourself."

I Want
ROOSEVELT
Again

"There are two more places that I want to take you on our field trip," said Mike. "One is inside and one is outside."

They went to a building. It was a museum. Inside they saw lots of pictures of Warm Springs a long time ago. They saw pictures of FDR in the pools. He was smiling.

"Look!" said Grant. "Look at all the kids. Do they have polio?"

"Yes they do," said his dad. "Many children with polio came to Warm Springs to try to get better. Some lived here until they were adults."

"That sounds sad," said Seve. He was puzzled. "If they had a disease and were crippled, then why are they all smiling?"

"Even FDR is smiling really big," said Weng-Ho. He pointed to a picture.

"Did FDR make them well?" asked Grant. "Is that what he gave them—a cure?"

Dad shook his head. "No. There was no cure for polio at that time. Today, kids get a vaccine so that they will not get polio. But back then, kids got crutches, or leg braces, or wheelchairs."

"That is so sad," said Seve.

"But they are all smiling," said Weng-Ho."

"This is a puzzle," said Grant.

Polio

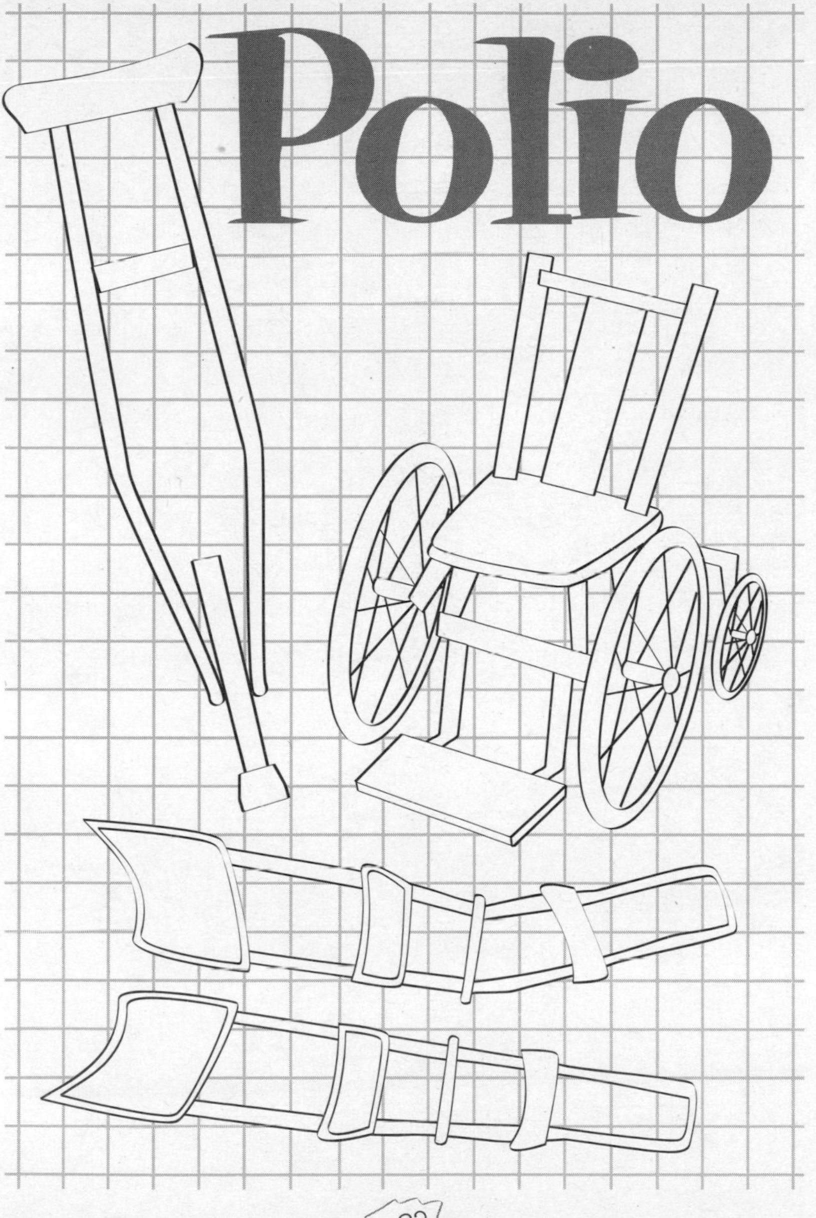

The Arrowhead

7 seven

The next place they went was to a small pool of warm water. They could see the warm spring flowing out of the mountain into the pool.

"This is where the Creek Indians used to live," said Mike. "They knew that the warm springs were good for your health. Sometimes, white travelers wanted to stop at the warm springs. A legend says that the Indians would let them pass in peace on their lands if they were coming to usc the warm springs."

"That was nice," said Grant.

“Yes, it was,” said his dad.

“But is a legend true or not true?” asked Seve.

“It is true or not true, as you believe it to be,” said Mike.

But Grant, Weng-Ho, and Seve were puzzled. What did all of this have to do with FDR? What did he give the people—the farmers and the kids with polio?

Suddenly, Weng-Ho shouted, “Look! I found an Indian arrowhead in the dirt! I think this must be an old Creek

Indian arrowhead!"

"That must mean that the legend is true!" said Seve. He looked around and soon he found an Indian arrowhead, too.

Now, Grant scrambled on the ground. He looked and he looked and he looked. Maybe Weng-Ho and Seve had found all the Indian arrowheads around here, he thought. Maybe he was out of luck. He felt sad.

Then, suddenly, his finger touched something in the red dirt. He thought it was probably just a rock. But it was an arrowhead. He smiled.

"I found one, too!" said Grant. "I hoped I would and I believed I would, and finally, I did!"

His dad just stood there and smiled.

"Hey, Dad!" said Grant. "That's the

answer to your puzzle, isn't it?"

"What answer?" asked Dad.

"What did FDR give the kids who had polio and the farmers who had no jobs or money?" said Seve. "That was the puzzle."

"Do you know the answer, Grant?" asked Weng-Ho.

"Yes, I do!" said Grant. "Hold out your Indian arrowheads."

The three boys held out their hands. The Indian arrowheads glistened in the sun.

"FDR gave the people HOPE," said Grant. "He gave them BELIEF that things would be better." He looked at his Dad.

Dad nodded. "Yes, he did. That is the answer to the puzzle."

"And were things better?" asked Weng-Ho.

Hope!
Belief!
Better!

Dad nodded again. “Yes, they were, boys,” he said. “Things are always better with hope and if you believe.”

“Well, I believe I’m hungry,” said Seve.

“I hope there is a cafe nearby,” said Weng-Ho.

“Lead the way, Dad!” said Grant. And thanks for the fun field trip!”

The End

The Puzzle of the INDIAN ARROWHEAD

A Little About FDR, Warm Springs, The Little White House, and Polio

When polio first became an epidemic in America, parents were very afraid. Since no one knew how you got "infantile paralysis," parents were afraid that if one child got polio, the others would be

infected, too. So, many parents brought the child with polio to Warm Springs and left him or her there. Often they did not even tell the child what they were doing or why. They hoped that Warm Springs could help their child, but mostly, they wanted to save their other children from this dreaded disease.

When FDR began to come to Warm Springs, he set out to make things better for all the people there with polio, especially the many children. He improved the

buildings, held holiday feasts, and most of all, spent time with the children playing in the pools. He truly did give them hope for their futures and the belief that they could lead a normal life.

In spite of what seems like a tragic era, when interviewed, many of the former patients at Warm Springs stress what a joyful time they had living there. Today, fortunately, there is a vaccine against polio. Warm Springs is still a fine place that treats patients and helps to rehabilitate them to as normal a life as possible.

three amigos
TM

About The Series Creator

Carole Marsh writes lots of books for kids. She started writing when she was just a kid. She is married to a cowboy named Bob. Carole likes to ride horses and figure out riddles, puzzles, and mysteries. Grant is her real-life grandson. Weng-Ho and Seve are his real-life amigos!

Glossary

arrowhead: a triangle-shaped piece of stone

disease: an illness that may or may not be contagious

FDR: 32nd president of the United States; elected to 4 terms

Great Depression: period in America following the Stock Market Crash of 1929 when many people lost their jobs and homes

iron lung: machine that some polio patients had to get inside to breathe

legend: story from the past, which may or may not be true

polio: also called infantile paralysis; disease of the lungs and limbs

New Deal: program that FDR created to help people get out of the Great Depression

vaccine: what your doctor may give you to prevent you from getting a disease

three amigos

Talk About It!

1. What is a field trip? Do you like to go on field trips? What is your favorite so far? Would you like to visit Warm Springs and The Little White House? Why or why not?

2. Was this field trip educational? Was it fun, too?

3. What did you learn about American history that you did not know before? How did this surprise you?

4. Would you have liked to have met FDR?

5. What does "handicapped" mean? What can it keep us from doing, if anything? What can we do even if we have a handicap?

6. Why is it important to get your vaccinations?

7. Have you ever found an Indian arrowhead? Would you like to find one?

8. What do you think Grant, Weng-Ho, and Seve learned on this field trip?

9. How important is it to have "hope" even when a situation is bad…and to believe that things can and will get better?

BRING IT TO LIFE!

1. Dress up like Indians! Use a paper bag to makc a vest. Cut a line down the middle of the front of the bag. Then, cut the bottom out of the bag. Cut armholes in the sides of the bag. Cut fringe along the bottom of the bag. Decorate it with your favorite colors! Use white paper or brown paper to make a headdress. First, cut a band to fit around your head. Then, make feathers to attach to the front of the band. Decorate and color the feathers. Attach them to the band, and fit the band around your head!

2. Map it Out! Find a map of Georgia. Find Warm Springs, Georgia on the map. What is the biggest city near Warm

Springs? List all the states you would have to travel through to get from your state to Georgia!

3. Do some research! Read about Franklin Delano Roosevelt. Get a piece of paper and answer these questions: Where was he born? Did he have any brothers and sisters? When was he first elected president? What was his wife's name? Did he have any pets when he was president? If so, what were their names?

4. Taste it! Roll out some sugar cookie dough. Cut arrowheads out of the dough and make arrowhead cookies! Decorate them with icing and candy pieces!

5. What can you do? Polio is a "communicable" disease, which means people can transfer it to one another. Many diseases are communicable. Make a list of things you can do to stop the spread of disease.

6. Bring in a guest speaker! Some of you may have grandparents or great-grandparents who were young adults when Franklin Roosevelt was president. Invite someone to talk to your group about what he was like!

LET'S LEARN ABOUT

ARROWHEADS!

Indian arrowheads are also known as "projectile points." There are many types of arrowheads. Many arrowheads were made of flint or other hard rocks. Other arrowheads were made from bone, antler tips, or copper.

Hunting arrowheads were usually shaped like an oval. This way they could easily be taken out of the prey. They were tightly fastened to the shaft. War arrowheads were often barbed. This means they had many sharp points.

Indians did not like to waste anything. Arrowheads that became dull were re-sharpened. Broken or worn arrowheads were often made into another tool like a knife!

Arrowheads were attached to the arrow by using tendons from animals or fibers from plants. Sometimes pitch from pine trees was used as glue.

It took great skill to make an arrowhead. Some people believe that the Indians considered them a work of art. Some Indians used other hard stones as hammers to chip the flint into shape. Others flaked pieces off with pieces of bone or antler.

Indian arrowheads are found in many places in the United States. Experts can usually tell where an arrowhead came from by the type of material used to make it.

Arrowheads are considered to be artifacts. Many are displayed in museums. Collectors also like to buy arrowheads and build up a big collection!

Hope!
Belief!

Better!

TECH CONNECTS

Hey, Kids! Visit
www.carolemarshmysteries.com to:

- JOIN THE CAROLE MARSH MYSTERIES FAN CLUB!
- GET A PICTURE OF FDR TO COLOR!
- GET AN ACTIVITY ABOUT THE LITTLE WHITE HOUSE!
- GET AN INDIAN ARROWHEADS ACTIVITY!

three amigos
TM